Petals

&

Gems

Fox Jones

Contents

Acknowledgments

Honestly, I didn't think this book or collection would see the light of day again. The poems in this book were originally published in my first collection Garden of Flower: A Visual Anthology. After being scammed by a publishing company, I wanted to throw all those poems away. It was too hurtful to even talk about them because of the experience. If it wasn't for some good people who pushed me to re-release these poems and to add some additional stories, this collection would have never been released. I want to thank the following:

To the Most High: Thank you for illuminating my path and allowing me to grow and have fun on this journey.

To Sheri: Thank you as my book project manager and mentor. Words can't express how much I appreciate everything.

To Alicia: Thank you for the feedback on the edits and the overall flow of the book. I know it was a trying time, but I appreciate all the work and love you put into my project.

To Latasha, Omari, and Shanetta: Thank you for your candor and your support. I wouldn't have had the courage to send this collection into the world without y'all. Blessings.

To Yas, Elizabeth, Keri, Mariana, Fatema, Tam, Erin, and Danielle: Your support has been overwhelming and I can't tell you how full my spirit has become. I truly love y'all.

To my sister, Keleigh: You're an amazing human being and your energy is unmatched. Let your love and light glow for the world to see and to feel. Love you to the moon and back.

To my sons Marquis, Aiden, and EJ: Thank you for being there for me and letting me be there for you as your mom. I'm honored and blessed to have you in my life.

To my rock, my love, my husband: Our rivers crossed, and we have merged into something so bountiful, there is only one word that can describe it: LOVE. May we continue to grow, flow, and merge together on this journey.

To the men and women of the Armed Forces: I'm inspired every day by y'all and I pray that each of you continue to inspire and aspire greatness.

To the reader: Once again, thank you for your support and faith in me. I'll never take any of it for granted.

Always,

Fox Jones

From The Desk of the CEO

Greetings!

If you are reading this, congratulations! You've been chosen to become a part of this organization. No matter your position, your contributions are key to our success.

There are so many ways to explain what we do and why we choose to follow this calling. Instead of telling you, I thought it would be best if the people who inspired us told you their stories.

You'll hear from both Flowers and Gems. Each one has a unique story; all I ask is that you listen with an open mind and remember.

Your mentors and trainers are here to guide you through this journey. Make sure you take advantage of the enormous wealth of knowledge they possess and are willing to instill.

Good luck with your training. We'll see you on the other side.

Nos Defendimus Aut Mori
Glacier
CEO, Deity Supreme Enterprises

Part 1: Petals

Introduction

I never understood flowers—
Their delicate petals
Their sensual fragrance
Beckoning…calling.
Wanting to be loved,
Longing to be held.
How something so magnificent,
Something so vulnerable
Can be so easily crushed.

How quickly we forget
The moment that flower made us feel alive—
Made us feel whole.
Made us feel wanted and loved.
How quickly our memory turns to dust
When that flower no longer holds us
In its enticing gaze.

We forget so often to take care of that flower.
The one that held us.
Attracted us.
Made us want more.
We take for granted its beauty.
Its grace.
Its magnetism.

You see, flowers come in different sizes,
Shapes, and colors.
Each one has different needs,
But…they all have the same need
To be loved. To be wanted. To be remembered.

These flowers…these 8 flowers
Are in different stages.
Some blossomed.
Others needed extra care.
Others are simply dying.

To know how to take care of a flower,
You must know the flower
To appreciate its beauty.
You need to know its beginning.

Come, stroll through the garden.
This garden full of life.
Stay awhile; learn something.
I have to warn you–all stories aren't pretty.
Some of the most beautiful flowers come from
The harshest of circumstances.

Listen to the story behind its growth.
Experience the reason for its beauty.

Are you ready?
Let's take a walk…

<u>*Innocence*</u>

Innocence is like spring—
Bringing hope and promise.
Innocence is like the dawn—
Beautiful and majestic.

Just like we treasure innocence,
We hold dear to the value of youth.
When we think of youth,
We think of how this thread in life's tapestry
Captures its essence.
Like a prized perfume,
Cherishing…holding onto the scent.
Clinging to the hope that someday
We can benefit from the extracts.

Violets and buttercups,
For centuries represented innocence and youth.
A fresh perspective.
Open minds and wide-open eyes.
These two flowers embody two spirits.
Unfortunately, these two spirits
Do not last forever.

All it takes is a significant moment,
Plucked from their bed.
Crushed and shattered dreams,
Never to be the same again.

Dark dreams now a part of the psyche

Snatches away any dreams or crystal visions.
In the end, it still leaves a trace.
A fragrance...of hope.

"Violet"

Long sleeves? Check.
Long skirt? Check.
Smiles? Check.
One last look in the mirror…okay.
Time to go to school…

It is really hot outside.
I have to walk in the heat.
The sweat is starting to pool.
Luckily, my skin is covered.
So no one can tell
Where the colors begin and end.

I know my parents love me,
And I am their world.
But what I don't understand
Is what I have done that was so terrible
That makes them want to hurt me.

Over and over, I promise to do better.
Over and over, I try really hard.
To not make the same mistakes,
But it seems like no matter how hard I try,
They only get madder.

I love my parents.
I would do anything to protect them.
We are a family.
All families go through hard times.
I don't want to be the reason for breaking up my family.

I don't have friends.

No one comes over to play.

We don't have people over.

We say it's because we like to keep to ourselves.

But honestly…I don't want anyone finding out our secret.

So, I'll keep it to myself,
Even if it means my family stays together.
I won't tell a soul,
Even if it means that I have to wear
Long sleeves…
Pants…
Long skirts…
And a smile for the rest of my life.

"Buttercup"

I took a shower,
Hoping to wash the shame away.
I cried a river of tears,
Trying to cleanse my soul of sin.
How could I let this happen?
Why didn't I see it coming?

I tried to eat,
Hoping that food would comfort me.
I tried to sleep,
But I kept waking to the apparitions that frighten me.
Why did this happen to me?

Was I that easy to become his prey?
He said he wanted me to tutor him.
Deep down, I felt special.
No one ever paid attention to me before
I was raised to be a good girl.

I can take care of myself…nothing is going to happen…
It felt funny at first—
His mouth…his hands.
It felt dangerous…forbidden.
His fingers went down my blouse and up my skirt.
He laid me down on his bed.
His weight pressed against mine.

Roaming
Tugging
Biting
My first time wasn't supposed to be like this.
I told him I had enough.
I told him to stop.

He laughed.
Called me a tease.
Called me a whore.
Said I was leading him on.
Told me he will finish what I started.
Told me to stop being a little girl.

I went numb.
Silence everywhere.
Shut my eyes,
Prayed it would be over soon.
A burning fierce pain enveloped me.
Virgin flesh torn apart.
The scent permeated the air.
I hated myself...I hated that moment.

I walked home.
Head down.
Ashamed and dirty.
Can anyone see me?
Does anyone know what happened?
I began to grieve my loss.

Who should I tell?
Not my mama...not my daddy.
They would just hang their heads in shame.

Should I tell God?
Where was He when I needed him?
Should I tell my friends?
No, they wouldn't understand.
No, this was my fault, and I was to blame.

I had to be strong.
I had to take responsibility.
I should not have been there.
My intentions were good,
But I should have known.
I told him…I screamed at him—
"No! Stop! It hurts! Please, stop!"

I should have known.
I should have never put myself in that situation.
I would not be reliving the nightmare over and over again.

I scrubbed myself hard…every night.
I cried hard…every night.
I prayed…every night.
I regretted…every night.
Because deep down…I knew it was my fault.

Grace

These two flowers…
Something special about these two flowers.
Used for their healing powers.
Inspired countless works of art.
Royalty has immortalized their petals
As national treasures.

Yet, the most forgotten,
Isolated…depending on the day.
No one truly understands the purpose
Or the grace of these two flowers.

And for that reason, they are often neglected.
When you hear the daffodils and the irises
Weave their tale,
Listen to their sorrow.
Feel their pain.
Never forget…

"Daffodil"

Bricks made of pain.
Mortar made of memories.
I keep building the wall higher and higher,
Wanting to protect those whom I love.
But these walls come down whenever you are near.

They crumble because of my belief in your lies.
They tumble because of my hope things will change.
Instead, you keep proving me wrong,
Shattering the myth of your repentance.

The defenders of my faith hold on as much as they can.
Fighting artillery fire.
Sometimes taking the bullet
In hopes that their defense is not in vain.
Some of them have died in their defense of me.

The defenders of my faith
Feel every punch.
Every verbal assault.
Every slap
Every pull
Every kick
Slam of the head.
They have heard my bones crack.
They saw my face drenched in blood and bruises.

Each time, they saw the cracks in the wall.
Every time, they helped me repair them.
Brick by brick…step by step…one day at a time
Only to be broken when you are near.
They are steadfast in their defense,
Conjuring a new battle plan,
Expecting to see victory.

I hire and fire generals,
"Believing" they will get it right.
 I sabotage their plans
Because of my love for you,
Or maybe I feel I don't deserve anything more.

I want this war to be over.
I am too weary to carry on.
I have no more strength.
I have none to give.
Maybe this was meant to be.
Maybe this was destiny.

The trumpet sounds.
The white flag is raised.
I lumber with hands high.

I surrender.

"Iris"

That night will forever haunt me.
The night my world turned upside down.
Images replay like a bad movie.
All carrying the same theme,
Hurt…pain…shame…guilt.

My shame has doubled.
I am constantly reminded of that night.
The night that I saw Anger.
The first time I have known Fear.
How do I live?

Tears fell…cleansing and soothing.
My soul, still troubled.
My mind, still conflicted.
Pictures like fractured glass,
Trying to piece together
What happened that night.

Serenity never comes.
I face an even greater choice—
Do I take a life to save my own?
It was not his fault.
That anger, hurt, and fear conceived him.
Should hate, shame, and guilt kill him?
That was not how I was raised.
This was not supposed to happen.
This only happens on TV.
This decision is too much to bear…help me!

Those who know my shame

Gave me their blessing.
This does not comfort my heart or my mind.
If I continue on this path,
I will hate the reminder of that night.
If I terminate,
I will live in purgatory for the rest of my life.

The sun has now set,
But the sky is filled with clouds.
I must breathe again.
Find a new life somewhere...somehow.
I don't want to do this...but I need to live.

I lie here empty—
Hollow and numb.
I realize it is gone.
Erased from my body,
But not from my memory...

<u>Loss</u>

Overcast skies.
Clouds filled with gray.
Tears water the earth,
Replenishing and calming its inhabitants.

We think of tears as a nuisance—
An inconvenience.
Until we see the beauty that comes from it.

Orchids were used as get well soon tokens.
Given to loved ones when mourning a loss.
Alleviating some of the sadness and suffering.

Today, this orchid is grieving.
She weeps as she tries to find comfort
For the love she lost.

"Orchid"

I thought of you today.
It wasn't very pretty.
The images in my mind
Haunted me of your untimely death.
Sharp pains stabbed my sides.
Agony and regret are my housemates.

You told me of your pain.
How you suffered in silence.
How you endured those touches…night after night.
How you lived in fear,
Praying there would not be another attack.

You told me that your sanity was disappearing.
How your spirit was slowly breaking.
How you could no longer hang on to the madness.

I thought of you today,
And of your pain.
How you wept in my arms,
Asking me to rescue you.
Asking me to believe you.
Wanting me to pull you from the precipice.

I knew you trusted me like no other.
No one could keep your secret.
No one else could be your shield…your blanket.
I felt your shame.

I felt your confusion.
You needed me.

But I walked away from you.
I walked away because I was not strong enough.
I walked away because I could not believe
A person could be so cruel to another.
I walked away because I didn't know what to do with the information you gave me.
I had a hard time believing God would allow this to happen.
I walked away because I didn't know how to swim
Or even throw a lifesaver.
I walked away because I could not rescue you.

I didn't know what to do.
I didn't know where to begin.
I didn't know where to go.
My unwillingness to become involved
Caused my body to shake with guilt and anguish.
Sleep eluded me…I could not reach out and do the right thing.
I wept endless tears
Because I lost my friend…my kin.
I cried because I was too late.
I cried because there was nothing I could do to bring you back.

No penance could bring back my mind.
No amount of prayer could ease my spirit.
Why did I not listen?

Why did I not just do something?!
Is this the price I paid for my silence?

Please forgive me, my friend…my kin.

Redemption

Gentle.
Fragile.
Soft.
How can something so delicate be so rigid?
Silence.
Bind.
Chained.
Gagged.
Something so beautiful shouldn't be so hard.
You see, objects adapt to their environment.
This flower here did not start as rough.
This blossom was full of promise.
Full of expectations.
But circumstances made her change her demeanor
From demure to aggressive.

Dreams and goals were snatched.
In that moment
Her petals fell to the ground.
She was in the garden,
Bare and without fruit.

Instead of withering.
Instead of vanishing.
She found a new life,
A new way…and became a better version of herself.

Ladies and gentlemen,
I present to you…Tiger Lily.

"Tiger Lily"

It is not our fault if we choose to bask in the glory of our own power.

It is not our fault that predators try to dismantle our state of mind.

Weak people do weak things.

There is no reason for what has been done.

You cannot convince me otherwise.

They think they are taking our power.
They think they are making us vulnerable.
They think this instance is going to
Cripple us.
Shame us.
Make us fall into submission.
They think we will go away...quietly.

No! No! No!
We are still standing!
We are still taking flight!
We are still breathing fire and air!
We are still moving mountains!
We will live!

You can't take something you never had.

You are upset that you can't scorch the earth like me.

You are angry that you can't make the constellations bow to your will.

You are upset...personally, I don't care why you are upset!

That how much you matter to me.
You wanted to silence royalty?
This is my truth!
The skies will hear about your revolt.
The earth will know who tried to dethrone me.
They will guarantee that you will pay for your crimes against humanity.
They will make sure that you know no peace…no solitude.

You have lost.
Your plan has failed.
May God have mercy on your soul.

Wisdom

Magnolias and gardenias.
Sought after for these things:
Beauty, grace, and elegance.
The wisest of flowers.
They have seen and been through it all.

Both are ancient flowers...but have very different opinions.
The magnolia is working class and headstrong.
The gardenia...upper class and refined.
Both are set in their ways...the same yet different.

A conversation between these two can be very interesting.
Listen closely to these grand dames of the garden...

"Gardenia"

Stella, guess what my granddaughter told me this morning?

She told me her husband, Darryl, had punched her last night.

Apparently, he's been beating her every single day

Since the wedding.

She told me it stopped while she was carrying their baby,

But as soon as that baby was born, he started right up again.

What'd I tell her?
I told her that she needed to be a good wife.
Stop nagging him.
He's going through some things.
The man has got to be strong in this world.
He don't need you pip-pipping him all the time.

Stella, you know for hundreds of years
The man is the head of the household.
Why should we go against thousands of years
Just because my granddaughter doesn't know when to be quiet?

Haven't you heard of stand by your man?
If you don't try to keep him, another woman will?

Don't give me that look!
You know your mother taught you the same thing!

What is so wrong with keeping house and home?

You know what?
The problem is that these young girls know nothing about sacrifice.
They want to jump ship as soon as times get hard.
What happened to for better or for worse?
Til death do us part?

Those aren't some lyrics in a song.
That, dear, is real life!
The sooner these young girls can understand that,
The better off they will be.

Sure, my husband, Harold, kept me in line.
I knew what I had to do.
I knew he loved me.
I knew he was a great provider
And a strong man.
All I had to do was my part.
Every now and then, I tried it.
But once I saw how much he loved me
I put away my childish behavior.

Stella, don't act all uppity now.
You know this is true!
Either way, I told my granddaughter to stay the course.
Quit trying to look for a way out.
Do your duty…as a woman, as a mother, and as a wife.

"Magnolia"

Bernice, I have always cherished our friendship.
And you have always had a strong mind.
But…as strong as you are, you are a fool!
Our culture, our community
Has carried this scar throughout the ages.

We, as women, are hurting.
We, as women, are sitting and standing by,
Watching…not moving
As our daughters suffer.
We are what our mothers feared we would become…
Complacent sheep.

Willing to accept any pain.
Any struggle.
As long as our men come home to us—
Wrong or right.
We will stand by them…because we are afraid.

Yes, Bernice!
I said it! We are afraid!
Afraid that we will not find love.
Afraid of not being accepted by our own.
Afraid that we are too old for change.
Afraid that if we do something different,
They will leave us with nothing.

We have perpetuated this myth, this story
That we are nothing without a man.

We have fueled this fire that no one will want us.

This is our lot in life; this is what we deserve.

You talk about girls taking their place...empower them!

All this foolishness about accepting a man's behavior!

Any man that beats on the one person who loves him is weak!

No real man would even think to beat a woman

Or even condone that type of behavior from his brethren!

Sacrifice? What is she to sacrifice?
Her pride? Her dignity? Her self-respect?
Wake up!

I love you, girl...but...you need to wake up.

Part 2: Gems

As we walk through the garden, you may notice a gem at the entrance of every section in the garden. The gem's mission is simple: to protect the flowers and guard the garden.

The elements choose the time, the place, and the materials to create a beautiful and powerful gem. And just like gems, it takes a special person to fulfill the garden's mission. The gems are fully committed to the protection and advocacy of all who have been wronged and all who don't have a voice.

To understand why people become gems, three have decided to graciously share the moments (the elements), which changed them, leading them to embark on a journey bigger than themselves, and in the hopes to inspire us to continue the path to our own growth and purpose.

May I present Ruby, Garnet, and Amethyst.

Ruby

When someone mentions New Orleans, it's usually about the rhythmic and soulful vibrations of our music, the different savory and sweet flavors of our food, or the mystical and magical religion known as voodoo. This city has a way of infiltrating all five of your senses to the point of yearning for a chance to experience it all over again, no matter where you're from or who you are. And even though the streets, buildings, and landscape look historically festive, and will lure the unsuspecting wanderer into a romantic fantasy of times past, the underbelly is so gritty and filthy even holy water wouldn't be able to remove the demonic stains.

New Orleans is a rare and enticing jewel, and while I love my city dearly, I feel trapped by the deep and dark happenings which go on in the shadows of that skyline. Between the humidity and the souls of those long gone who haunt me from the grave, I needed to get away and start fresh. I joined the Army after I graduated high school to escape. The move unlocked my potential, and I flourished. I promoted a few times and found friends that weren't as fucked up as me. I was able to pretend my past didn't exist and become a new person altogether. Until it all came crashing down one fateful evening.

I got home after a long day filled with whining soldiers and old men past their prime telling me how to do my job. I plopped the day's mail on my kitchen table and poured myself a rum and coke. As the liquor found its way to my veins, I sifted and browsed through the mail. A faint scent of lilac tickled my nose. Only one person in my life wore lilac perfume, and I instantly knew the letter was from my mother. After all these years, her cursive handwriting was still beautiful and delicate, just like the scent that she loved to wear.

I opened the envelope and unfolded the letter, which contained a poem and an apology:

Oh my God.
I can't believe this is happening.
Why did this happen?
How did this happen?

My daughter.
My pride and joy.
I had so many hopes and dreams for her
And now this?!

I explained to her about boys.
How they're no good.
How all they want is one thing,
And yet, this happens!

Now, my pristine daughter is nothing but a slut!
What am I going to tell my friends?
How are we going to look?
What are we going to say?
The shame of it all!

What was she doing over at his house?
Why was she even talking to him?
Tutoring?! Can't believe she fell for that!

She said she was raped...I don't believe her!
If she wasn't at his house, this wouldn't have happened!

She seemed fine that day.
She's got to be lying.
If she was truly raped, she wouldn't be able to eat.
She wouldn't be able to sleep.
I've seen rape victims before...
And she doesn't look that way to me.

Why did she do this to me?
Where did I go wrong?
How did I fail?
I tried...Lord knows I tried.

I'm so sorry I didn't believe you. I'm so sorry I wasn't the mother you needed me to be. I tried to make up for it, and I hope you will forgive me. I'm so sorry.
   Mama

  Remember when I said ghosts still haunt me? This is the main one. I wanted to forget my cousin raped me at 15 years old. We were in the same high school literature class, and he claimed he needed some help with a story we studied. I had no idea he had something else in mind. After the incident, I went home and tried to go on with my life as normally as I could. Unfortunately, my mama heard about it from the news, a.k.a our neighbor. She confronted me, called me all kinds of names, and beat the crap out of me. She claimed she was trying to get the lustful demons out of my body because only a demon would make me want my own 18-year-old cousin. We never spoke again.

  As I reread the letter, a wave of anger, guilt, and confusion washed over me. Anger toward her because she didn't believe me, guilt because of the act, and confusion because I had no idea what she was talking about with, "tried to make up for it".

As I struggled to decipher my mama's apology, my phone rang. I let out a groan and rolled my eyes as I picked up the phone.

"Hello?" I rubbed my hand on my forehead, trying to stop a headache from taking shape. I held my mouth to suppress a squeal when I heard Ms. Antoinette's voice on the other end. We chatted, but I could tell something was off with my Muh Dear. When I heard the exhaustion and sorrow in her voice, I knew this wasn't going to be a pleasant call.

Hesitantly, I told her about the letter from Mama. I listened to her insert a grunt here and there, but she didn't say anything. After I finished, my grandmother let out a fatigued sigh, and the gates opened wide with some new information. She let me know my mama was in prison for exterminating my cousin. I massaged my temple as my grandmother recounted the events that happened a month ago. Apparently, at a party my mama hosted, my cousin confessed to raping me and countless other sexually explicit crimes against young girls in the community. According to Muh Dear, my mama saw my cousin laugh about the situation. My mama abruptly grabbed a wine bottle, broke it, and stabbed him repeatedly as he bled out on the floor. My cousin's mama called the police and snitched on my mama. Since my mama was covered in blood, she sat down on the floor against the wall and waited. My mama, voluntarily, turned herself in and waived a trial, hence, the reason why she's in prison. The dead silence between me and Muh Dear filled the air, and I tried to process the information. I took a couple of sips of my drink and tried to process the information. The anger and hate bubble in my chest popped. In its place is now a sorrow and compassion bubble. This piece of news was too much to take in one night.

I mindlessly listened to Muh Dear as she tried to convince me to forgive my mama and stay in touch with her. I know my grandmother means well, but that wound runs deep and refuses to heal. I know one day I will talk with my mama and forgive her, but right now, it's not the time and I don't feel led by the saints or the ancestors to move forward in that direction. Before we hung up for the night, Muh Dear asked me to take in my niece, Bernadette, since my mother is in prison. My sister died due to street violence and my mama took care of Bernadette until this incident. Since she's my favorite niece, I, begrudgingly, complied.

Raising my niece away from New Orleans helped calm the ghosts but didn't make them entirely disappear. Occasionally, those ghosts disturbed me throughout my career. And no matter how far I ran, they always found me. My city's underbelly and the military underskirts share the same dirt. Seeing what happened to the perpetrators incensed me. If you had some sort of connection, nothing happened to you. Plus, it was usually white men who were able to become chameleons and be reborn into something else.

Two years after retirement, my best friend, Minerva, came to see me and proposed a business plan about the organization. All the ins and outs concerning operations and logistics. Most importantly, she laid out how the network could help those who felt betrayed by the system, both military and civilian. I thought about my mother. I thought about my niece. I thought about all the ghosts who haunted me. Finally, I thought about myself.

It's been years since the ghosts visited me. Now, we have operatives and associates around the world, ensuring the organization's mission remains the same: *nos defendimus aut mori* – We defend or die. I've found my purpose, and I will defend all the people who couldn't defend themselves—or die.

Garnet

I was one of those soldiers who would yell HUA instead of answering yes or no. Like any soldier, I took pride in my ability to adapt to any situation ranging from an outbreak of war to someone having a heart attack. Trust me, I was ready. Yet, with all my years and experience in the military, one specific event shook the foundations I believed the military stood for.

It was only seven years ago, but I remember it as if it happened yesterday. I'd just graduated from the First Sergeant Academy and deployed the following month with my new unit as their First Sergeant. Words couldn't describe how excited I was because these opportunities were rare. Usually, my leadership would want you to cut your teeth in garrison. but being chosen for this particular assignment proved how much the top brass had so much faith and trust in me and my abilities.

When I arrived, it was a sweltering and fast paced environment. Every day was filled with sweat and lots of sunscreen, along with grumbling and mumbling about air conditioners not working and failed internet connections where troops couldn't call home or play video games. I even had to break up a few fights. On top of all of that, I had to advise the commander and the senior enlisted leader on issues that might affect the morale and discipline of the troops throughout the command. Constantly, I had to be vigilant. The work was tiring but rewarding because I got to reap the benefits of the outcome. Happy troops plus high morale equals a very ecstatic commander. This deployment was going to be a cakewalk...or so I thought.

I completed the barracks check and needed to take a breather. I walked outside and the sky looked amazing. I was thinking about life in general when I heard some rhythmic plodding coming up behind me. The huffing got closer, and my ears perked up. I whirled around to see the Operations Chief, Master Sergeant Billings, running toward me. I was surprised to see panic on the face of someone who had a reputation of being unflappable. She pointed in a direction and took off. Instinctively, I followed her. As we ran by buildings, she described a scene so horrific you would have thought she copied the details from a horror novel.

We arrived at the clinic and were greeted by the emergency room doctor. His face was grey and somber as he briefed us the necessary details on what happened. Master Sergeant Billings and I went to go see our troop. My blood ran cold when I saw her. My troop was crying through swollen eyes and a busted lip. She was bloody and beaten like a pulverized orange. Her voice cracked as she screamed one question: why? Her blood was everywhere. She had to be restrained because she was inconsolable. I looked over at my Chief and saw tears run down her cheeks and chin. All she could do was grasp the troop's hand with both of hers and touch her forehead to hers. It was the first time in my career that I felt helpless.

I stood back and surveyed the scene. So many questions ran through my mind. What in the actual fuck? Who would do this? Why would they do this? So much blood. I put a reassuring hand on my Chief's shoulder. I prayed to the ancestors to watch over all three of us. While I prayed, the medics took the troop to the back for more tests and a possible operation to repair her jaw.

The next day, the commander, senior enlisted leader, Master Sergeant Billings, and I gathered to read the police and hospital report to discuss the next steps. A ball of distress, grief, and rage grew from my stomach to my eyes as I read the report, which included the victim's statement. It was a brutal assault, complete with excruciating details of the encounter. The hospital report described her various injuries, including a broken eye socket, broken nose, bruised vocal cords, and many broken ribs. Once the commander and the senior enlisted leader read the reports, they told us the case was turned over to base leadership with the military police investigating. The only thing we could do was cooperate with the authorities and not discuss the case with anyone.

While we tried to keep the news from spreading, it was inevitable the command would find out and choose sides. As much as I tried to protect the victim, I couldn't be there with her all day, every day. The victim endured so much hate and bullying and it started to affect me. The hospital scene replayed in my head so many times that I couldn't sleep for two days. So much blood. All I could see was the blood and her face. Who could hate someone that much to fuck up someone beyond recognition?

The five guys who were responsible for the assault were found not guilty by the military panel. Even with all the evidence, they treated the five soldiers as if it was the command's fault that we inconvenienced them by holding them accountable. The same panel treated the victim as if the assault was her fault. From what my birdie told me, Master Sergeant Billings was kicked out of the room because she was the only one who stood up for her and was the only one who called them on their bullshit.

I needed some peace and needed to talk about what happened without judgment. I didn't seek out Master Sergeant Billings because she had other things going on. I decided to go to the unit chaplain. At least with the chaplain I had total confidentiality, even if I had to listen to a little bit of the Blessed Virgin and Her Son, sprinkled with some good advice.

A couple of years after confessing my sins and asking for forgiveness, I retired from the United States Army. After the uniform, I still lived with the knowledge of someone who had been assaulted on my watch and I couldn't do anything to help. Day after day, I played the scenario in my head and wondered what I could have done differently. I was in a deep and dark place. I wanted a chance to redeem myself and help others who have been in this space and didn't have anywhere to turn.

One day, out of nowhere, retired Sergeant Major Billings recruited me to work for the organization. I worked my way through the ranks as an operative and now I'm the Security Manager. I evaluate future operatives and analysts to ensure we hire the best of the best to clean up the messes left by the military justice system and the civilian justice system whether that is to rehabilitate the perpetrators or exterminate. The organization has given me new life and a way to forgive myself. I know no one is perfect, but we can damn guarantee that justice will be served.

Amethyst

If you need to know anything about me, just know that I hate bullies. Not just any bully. The type of bully who looks good on paper and looks perfect in pictures but knows how to inflict the most damaging injury while making the bruise invisible. What's funny is when you get the courage to speak up or report, your leadership tends to look the other way. They only engage when they no longer look good and must answer for the flaw. No one likes to be called out due to a flaw, so they try to cover it up so the machine can still operate at full capacity. If the machine is operational, they look good. These are the same people who swear they believe in God even though they can't see Him but are unwilling to believe you when you want to report a bully because they don't see the trauma the bullies have caused.

My earliest memory of being bullied happened in middle school. My social studies teacher instructed the class to bring a baby picture for an assignment. I brought my favorite picture because my bottom two teeth and my dimples showed. My mom warned me not to bring it, but I insisted because it was my favorite. While I was helping the teacher in class, two girls stole my picture and wrote Tar Baby on my face in bold pink permanent marker. They passed the picture around and some of my classmates laughed. A male classmate remarked I would have been prettier if I wasn't so dark. The comments by my classmates and the comment on my picture made me so ashamed I couldn't bring myself to submit the picture or tell my teacher what happened. Because I refused to discuss with my teacher what happened or submit the marked-up photo for a grade, she gave me a zero for the assignment. Later that day, I got a beating from my mom because not only did I lose my baby picture, but I also got a zero for the assignment.

I thought the bullying would stop once I became an adult. Instead, while I served in the military, I was ostracized by my male and female peers due to my strong bearing. They would express their "fear" of me to supervisors and leadership. I was constantly reprimanded because my body language betrayed my thoughts or when I spoke, my voice wasn't full of flowers and peppermints. I was astonished when a male peer displayed the same assertive attitude and was praised, but when I exhibited the same behavior, I was vilified.

As time flew by, I learned it was easier to make myself uncomfortable so others could feel at ease. I made a conscious effort to speak in a lower and softer tone. I would look down instead of looking directly in the eye. I used my intimate experience in disguising pain as a defense mechanism many times. I became numb to bullying. Although I shielded myself with this technique, and people assumed I was okay, the pain from the wounds sometimes became unbearable. The pain was a constant reminder that I wasn't good enough and never will be good enough. Until one day, I had enough.

I was working on paperwork in my office when I received a phone call to see the commander. I locked my computer and went to the work center. When I arrived, I remember being surprised because the commander was there with other officers and civilians. The deputy commander, without warning, cussed me out in front of everyone. He called me everything from lazy to incompetent over a task that wasn't completed. The task wasn't even assigned to my department, but he felt we should've kept oversight. As I absorbed the barrage of verbal venom—not one person came to my aid. I slowly sensed my spirit retreating into my shell, and all I could muster was a smile. And as I smiled, I noticed how everyone allowed him to continue to talk to me disrespectfully, but no one stopped him. Once he was finished with his tirade, I whispered, "we'll fix it."

As I walked out of the area and went back to my office, the ceiling and floor became blurred. I grabbed my keys and my cover and walked swiftly to my car. I popped open the trunk and pulled out an aluminum baseball bat I kept for safety reasons. I strolled back into the building as I made my way to the deputy commander's office. His door was open, and I knocked with a solid thud. The baseball bat was behind my back. He looked up and demanded to know if I'd fixed the issue. I closed the door, walked over to him, and swung my bat to meet his shoulder. The blow knocked him to the floor. I stood over him and hammered his kneecaps. As he writhed and screamed in pain, my heart danced in delight, and I swung harder. I screamed at him to apologize as I moved from his kneecaps to his ribs and back. The room grew hotter as people stood behind me and yelled for me to stop, yet no one took the bat out of my hands. I only stopped to catch my breath and to survey my handiwork. I smiled as I threw the bat down. I strutted past the astonished crowd. I felt so much better, even when I was arrested outside the building. I didn't even care. One thing's for sure: that mofo will never disrespect me again.

The charges were dismissed, but I was kicked out of the military with a general discharge. As I finished the paperwork to leave the unit, no one from my leadership even had the balls to say goodbye. They turned their backs on me, even though I was justified in beating that mofo's ass. I walked out of that building as if Atlas removed the world from my shoulders. I caught myself smiling in the rearview mirror. It's been a while since I'd smiled. I didn't even look back or shed a tear when I drove away from the base for good.

After a couple of years living off the grid, the only friend I had left contacted me. When I was kicked out, she was the only one who checked in on me and we talked from time to time. Now, she's out of the military and making a decent living as a case manager and analyst. From what she's told me, they look at discharge cases and correct errors due to ignored or mishandled circumstances by the military justice system or the civilian justice system. She told me she was assigned to my case and was researching the events. I was more than happy to detail the events that led to my discharge. As I retold the most painful events, I felt her listening to me and her genuine concern. I heard her keyboard clacking away but it didn't distract me from telling my story. After a three-hour conversation, she gave me her number and a number to a therapist who worked with veterans like me. Before we hung up, she asked me what I would like to see happen. This was a deep, yet simple question and I had to pause. I gulped down some air and told her I want my discharge to be upgraded to honorable because I didn't get a fair shake. She replied, "justice was coming" and hung up the phone.

Two months later, justice came in the form of a letter which stated my discharge had been upgraded from general to honorable with my new benefits. I cried as I read the letter. This one thing made my outlook on the world a lot brighter. My good fortune continued to run a week later because my friend called to let me know there was an opening at her job as an analyst and requested my resume so she could submit it.

It's been five years now and I love my job. I get to put bullies back in their place without having to place myself in an uncomfortable position or having to second guess my steps. I feel proud I get to help those who have been in similar situations as me and finally receive justice. Sometimes I need to get dirty to complete the job but that's a small price to pay for the reward. No longer will the bullies get to look good on paper and pictures and get away with their crimes. No longer will leadership be able to sweep the transgressions under the rug so the machine can continue to operate. A new day has come. All will come to light.

Conclusion

We have now reached the edge of the garden.
This doesn't mean the journey is complete.
As you can see,
There are many more species here.
Each wanting to be loved.
Each wanting to belong.

This garden is their community.
Each flower and gem have a soul.
Every petal and every glint tell a story.

Beauty and ugliness exist in this garden.
One cannot exist without the other.
Now…the real question is…what are you going to do?
Listen to their stories and continue to grow through your experiences?
Or shut the gates and cease to exist?
The choice is yours.